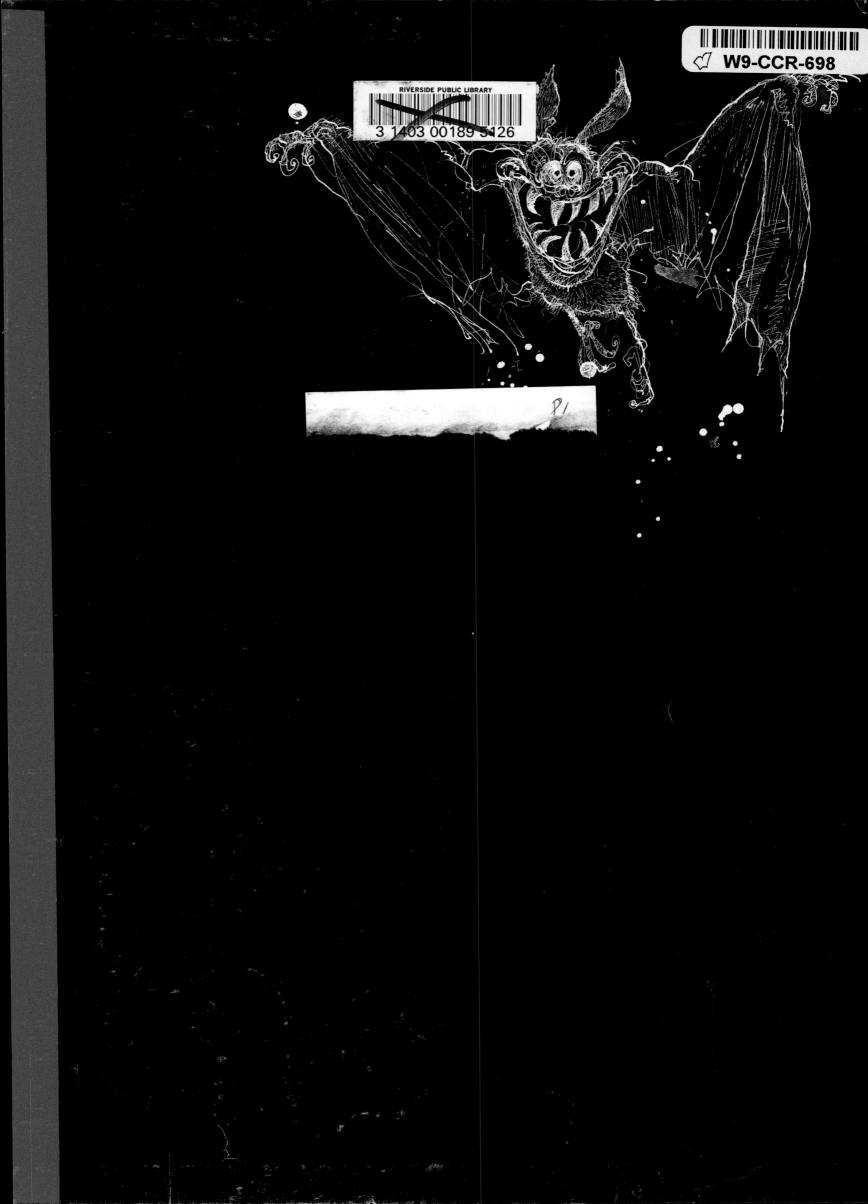

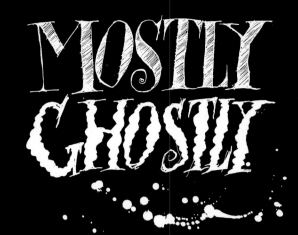

AS
I was GOING UP the stair
I met a man Who WASN'T there.
He WASN'T there AGAIN today
oh, how I wish he'd GO AWAY.

Anonymous

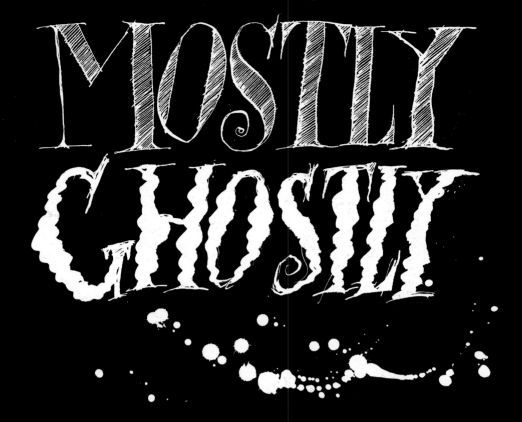

MOSTLY GHOSTLY

ADAPTED BY STEVEN ZORN FROM STORIES BY
Ambrose Bierce ~ F. Marion Crawford
Sir Arthur Conan Doyle ~ Washington Irving
M. R. James ~ Richard Middleton
Edith Nesbit ~ Barry Pain

ILLUSTRATED BY JOHN BRADLEY

COURAGE
BOOKS
AN IMPRINT OF
RUNNING PRESS
PHILADELPHIA, PENNSYLVANIA

Contents

Copyright © 1991 by Running Press.
Illustrations © 1991 by John Bradley
All rights reserved under the Pan-American and International Copyright Conventions.

This book may not be reproduced in whole or in part in any form or by any means, electronic or mechanical, including photocopying, recording, or by any information storage and retrieval system now known or hereafter invented, without written permission from the publisher.

Canadian representatives: General Publishing Co., Ltd., 30 Lesmill Road, Don Mills, Ontario M3B 2T6.

International representatives: Worldwide Media Services, Inc., 115 East Twenty-third Street, New York, NY 10010.

9 8 7 6 5 4 3 2

Digit on the right indicates the number of this printing.

Library of Congress Cataloging-in-Publication Number 91-71087

ISBN 1-56138-033-4

Edited by **Gregory C. Aaron**

Design and art direction by **Alastair Campbell**

Cover illustration by **John Bradley**
John Bradley is represented by Folio, 10 Gate Street, Lincoln's Inn Fields, London WC2A 3HP.

Printed in Hong Kong by South Sea International Press.

Published by Courage Books, an imprint of Running Press Book Publishers, 125 South Twenty-second Street, Philadelphia, Pennsylvania 19103.

Introduction

*I*t's a rainy, moonless night. You're lying in bed, reading your favorite scary story. No one else is home.

Suddenly the lights go out. The darkness is total, except for fiery flashes of lightning. Weird, shadowy shapes dance upon the ceiling and climb down the walls.

What's that sound? Is someone rapping on your bedroom window? You tell yourself it's probably just the wind rattling a tree branch. At least that's what you hope it is. Do you dare to turn and look?

Nothing is better than a good, old-fashioned tale of terror. It's fun to feel the goose bumps that rise on your arms as you read about ghosts and monsters. What is more exciting than a visit to the world of the unknown – as long as you're back by dinnertime?

If you love being frightened, you're not alone. Storytellers have been inventing spooky tales for a very long time, and people have always been eager to listen.

This book is a collection of eight classic chillers – a creepy collection of roaming ghosts and haunted places, horrible events and unsolved mysteries. Also included are a few chuckles, just to remind you that it's fun to be frightened.

So draw the blinds, dim the lights, and find a comfortable chair. Your adventure is about to begin. Enjoy it!

Steven Zorn

ON THE BRIGHTON ROAD

Richard Middleton

Slowly the sun climbed, revealing a sparkling world of snow. There had been a hard frost during the night, and a cold wind blew fine, snowy dust from the trees.

A tramp was asleep at the side of the road. He struggled for a moment with the snow that covered him. Then he sat up, surprised.

"What! I thought I was in bed," he said to himself. "And all the while I was out on the road."

He stretched his arm and legs, and shook the snow off himself. As he stood, the cold wind made him shiver.

"I suppose I'm lucky to wake at all in this. I could have been frozen in my sleep."

He started walking along the road with his back turned to the hills. Soon he overtook a boy standing on the road. The boy had no overcoat, and he looked unspeakably fragile against the snow.

"If you don't walk too fast, I'll come a bit of the way with you," the boy said. "It's a bit lonesome walking this time of day."

The tramp nodded.

"I turned eighteen last August," said the boy. "I've been on the road six years."

"I dropped by the roadside last night and slept where I fell," said the tramp.

"It's a wonder I didn't die."

The boy looked at him sharply.

"How do you know you didn't?" replied the boy.

"I don't understand," admitted the tramp.

"You haven't been a tramp as long as I have," said the boy hoarsely. "People like us belong to the road. We can't ever escape from it. Even if we die,

"I've been on the road for six years, and do you think I'm not dead?" the boy asked. "I was drowned bathing at Margate, and I was killed by a gypsy with a spike. He knocked my head right in. And twice I froze like you last night. And I was hit by a car on this very road. And yet I'm walking along here now because I can't help it. Dead! I tell you we can't get away if we want to."

The boy broke off in a fit of coughing. The tramp paused while he recovered.

"You'd better borrow my coat for a bit, your cough's pretty bad."

"You don't understand at all, do you?" the boy said fiercely. He collapsed suddenly, and the tramp caught him in his arms.

The tramp looked down the road. A car flashed in the distance and came smoothly through the snow.

"I'm a doctor," said the driver as he pulled up. "What's the trouble?" He listened to the boy's strained breathing.

"Pneumonia," he declared. "I'll give him a lift to the hospital. You, too, if you'd like."

"I'd rather walk," said the tramp.

The boy winked faintly as they lifted him into the car. "I'll see you later," he said softly to the tramp.

All morning the tramp splashed through the thawing snow. Then he found a lonely barn in which to fall asleep. It was dark when he woke. He started trudging once again through the slushy roads.

He hadn't gone far when a frail figure slipped out of the darkness to meet him.

"If you don't walk too fast, I'll come a bit of the way with you," said a familiar voice. "It's a bit lonesome walking this time of day."

"But the pneumonia!" cried the tramp.

"I died this morning," said the boy.

SELECTING A GHOST

Sir Arthur Conan Doyle

I had always wanted to live in a castle. So, when I saw one advertised, I couldn't resist. It was a mansion called Goresthorpe Grange.

It had almost everything – slits along the stairs to shoot arrows through, equipment for pouring molten lead upon the heads of visitors – even a moat. These were certainly charming features, but something was missing. Goresthorpe Grange did not have a ghost.

I am a firm believer in the supernatural, and I assumed that a castle as old as the Grange would have at least one ghost. Sadly, I was wrong.

For a long time I hoped against hope. Every strange sound would send a thrill through me. Could these noises be ghosts? But no. There was always some other explanation.

How I longed to hear those moans and wails of some restless spirit in my home! How unfair that my neighbor's house was haunted by a perfectly respectable ghost, and he didn't even appreciate it.

Finally, I could take no more. I had to get a ghost for the Grange. But how? My reading taught me that most ghosts are the result of a crime. I asked my butler if he wouldn't mind sacrificing himself, or murdering someone else for the sake of getting a ghost. He wasn't amused at all.

"I know," said my wife, Matilda, one day. "We must have a ghost sent down from London. My cousin, Jack Brocket, could help us."

This cousin of Matilda's was a clever young man who made his living doing odd jobs. I had to admit that finding a ghost was about as odd as a job could be.

The next day at noon I visited Mr. Brocket's office. The door was opened by an assistant who seemed amazed to see a real client.

"Let me get this straight," said Mr. Brocket after I gave him my request. "You want me to find a ghost for Goresthorpe Grange?"

"Quite so," I answered.

"Easiest thing in the world," he replied cheerfully. "Excuse me a moment."

Jack ran up a ladder and began rummaging through a pile of books on a high shelf.

"Here it is!" he cried, jumping off the ladder with a crash. "Page 41.

Just chuck yourself down there, old chap!

'Christopher McCarthy,'" Jack read. "'Weekly seances – attended by all the important spirits of ancient and modern times. Nativities, charms, abracadabras, messages from the dead.' He may be able to help us," Jack said. "However, I'll look further and see if I can get a cheaper price."

Jack said he would send me a letter when he had news. There was nothing else to do but go home and patiently wait to hear from him.

A letter came after a few days. "Am on the track," wrote Jack. "Professional spiritualists not helpful, but I met a fellow in a pub yesterday who says he can get a ghost for you. His name is Abrahams, and he'll be down next week."

I impatiently awaited the arrival of Mr. Abrahams. I could hardly believe that a mortal could have power over the spirit world. Still, I had Jack's word.

Jack's word was good. One evening a carriage pulled up. I hurried down to meet Mr. Abrahams. I half expected an assortment of ghosts to be crowded into the carriage with him.

Abrahams was a sturdy, pudgy little fellow, with keen, sparkling eyes and a wide, good-humored grin. All he had with him was a small leather bag. He greeted me and my wife, who had just joined us.

I led him upstairs, where a meal was waiting. He carried his little bag with him. As he walked, his little eyes rolled around and around, noticing every piece of furniture he passed.

When the table was cleared, Mr. Abrahams got down to business.

"So you want a ghost?" he asked. "Well, you won't find a better man for the job than me. Just me and my bag."

"You don't mean to say that you carry ghosts about in bags!" I remarked.

Mr. Abrahams smiled. "You wait," he said. "Give me the right place and the right hour — and this here essence of Lucoptolycus — and you'll have your choice of ghosts."

He pulled a small vial from his vest pocket. It contained a colorless liquid. "We begin at ten minutes to one in the morning," he continued. "Some say midnight. But at ten to one there's a better selection of spirits."

Mr. Abrahams rose to his feet. "And now, suppose you show me 'round the house and let me choose the best room for the haunting. Some rooms are better than others."

The little man carefully inspected every room and corridor. Finally, he stopped in the banquet hall.

"This here's the place!" he said, dancing around the table like a little goblin. "There's plenty of room for ghosts to glide in here. Leave me alone to prepare the room, and at half-past twelve come in."

I went downstairs to the room beneath, to sit with my wife. Through the ceiling we could hear Mr. Abrahams pacing the floor, trying to lock the door, and dragging a heavy piece of furniture in the direction of the window. I heard the rusty creak of the hinges as the window opened. My wife thought she could hear

Mr. Abrahams speaking in low whispers. He was probably summoning spirits. I was impressed.

At half-past twelve I went upstairs to see my visitor. There were no signs that the furniture had been moved.

"You shall drink the essence of Lucoptolycus," said Mr. Abrahams. "Whatever you may see, speak not and make no movement, or else you'll break the spell."

I sat where he told me. Mr. Abrahams took a piece of chalk and drew a half-circle around us on the floor. Around the edge of the half-circle he drew mysterious figures. Then he uttered a long stream of strange words and pulled out the bottle of Lucoptolycus for me to drink. The liquid had a faintly sweet odor. I paused before drinking it, but then downed it in a gulp. It didn't taste bad. I felt no change come over me. I leaned back in my chair and waited for what was to come.

Mr. Abrahams chanted some more. I began to feel pleasantly warm and drowsy. Beautiful thoughts drifted through my head. Just as I was about to doze, the door at the far end of the room opened.

It swung slowly back upon its hinges. I sat up in my chair, clutching the arms. I stared with a horrified glare at the dark passage. Something was coming. Dim and shadowy, I saw it flit across the threshold. A blast of ice-cold air swept down the room, chilling my very heart.

A voice like the wind said: "I am the invisible presence. I am here but not here. I cause shivers and breathe sighs. I kill dogs. Choose me."

I was about to speak, but the words choked in my throat. The shadow flitted across the hall and vanished in the darkness.

I turned my eyes to the door once more. To my astonishment, a small old woman hobbled into the hall and crouched at the edge of the chalk circle. Her face was hideous. I shall never forget it.

"Ha! ha!," she screamed, raising her hands like claws. "I am the fiendish old woman. My clothes are filthy. I curse people. I am hated. Shall I be thine, mortal?"

As I tried to shake my head, she swung at me with her crutch and vanished with a scream.

The instant she was gone, in walked a tall and noble man. His face was deadly pale, and surrounded by a fringe of dark hair that fell in ringlets down his back. He was dressed in yellow satin and a sword hung from his hips. He crossed the room in majestic strides.

"I am the cavalier," he remarked in a smooth voice. "I pierce and am pierced. I clink steel. This is a bloodstain over my heart. I work alone, or with shrieking damsels."

He bowed and then vanished.

He had hardly gone before a feeling of intense horror stole over me. The room filled with an invisible but ghastly creature. In a quavering and gusty voice it said, "I am the leaver of footsteps and the spiller of blood. I tramp upon corridors. I make strange and disagreeable noises. I snatch letters and place invisible hands on people's wrists. I burst into peals of hideous laughter. Shall I do one now?"

Before I could say anything, a loud and awful bellow echoed through the room. Then the creature disappeared.

My eyes turned automatically to the open door. Once again I was frozen by the horrible sight that appeared next.

It was a very tall man, if it might be called a man. Thin bones poked through its rotting flesh. It was gray in color. A sheet was wrapped around the figure, forming a hood over its head. Two fiendish eyes peered out, blazing like red-hot coals. The lower jaw hung down, revealing a shriveled tongue and black and jagged fangs.

"I am the American blood-curdler," it said in a hollow voice. "Look well at my blood and my bones. I am grisly and sickening. I can turn hair white in a night."

The monster stretched out its fleshless arms to me. I shrunk back. The creature vanished, leaving behind a sickening, repulsive odor. I was having second thoughts about selecting a ghost for my home. I prayed that was the last of the hideous parade.

A faint sound of rustling clothes alerted me that another phantom was on its way. I looked up. A young and beautiful woman floated in. She wore the fashion of a bygone day. Her face showed

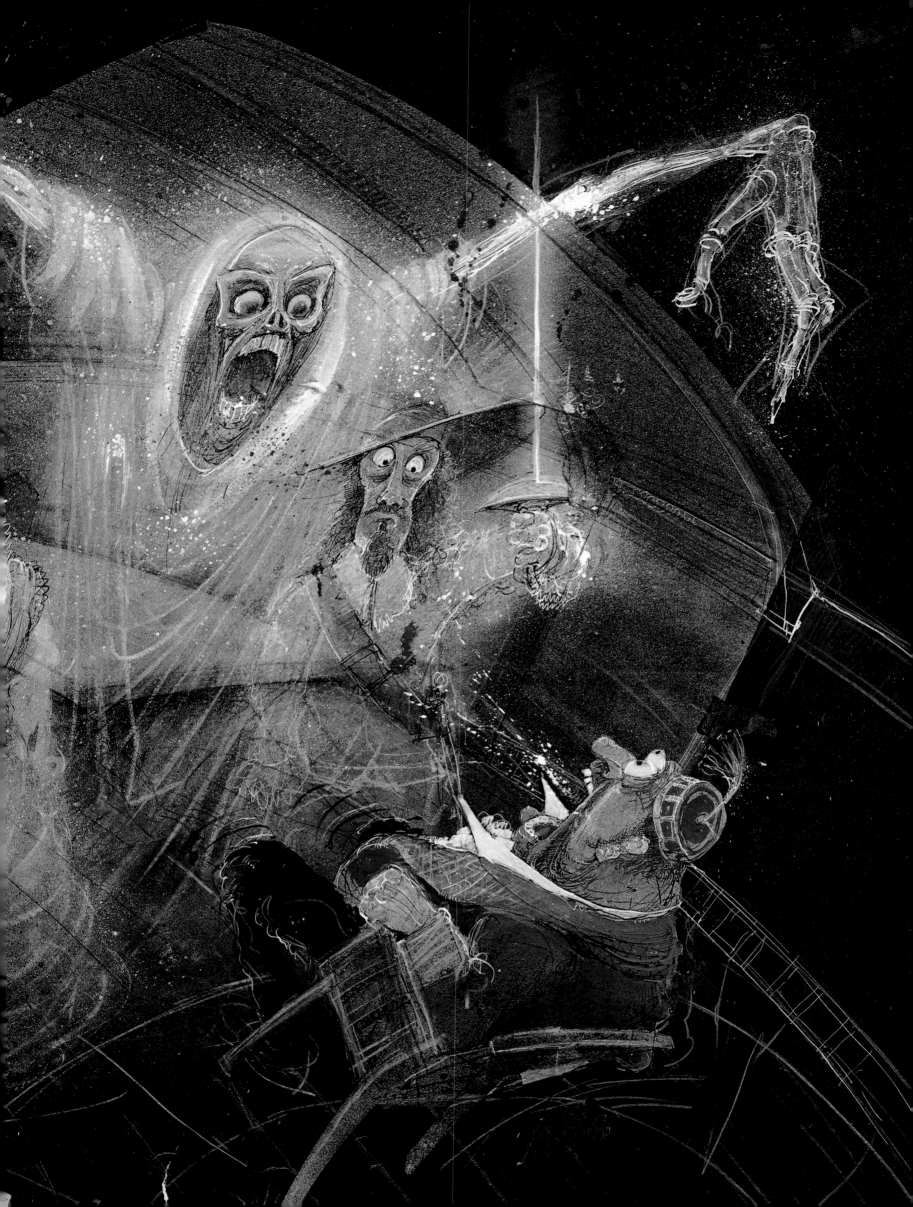

traces of passion and suffering. She crossed the hall with a gentle sound, and then, turning her lovely and sad eyes to me, she said:

"I am beautiful and ill-treated. I have been cheated and forgotten. I shriek at night and glide down passages. I have very good taste. Will you not choose me?"

Her lovely voice died away and she smiled as she faded before my eyes. That smile settled the matter.

"She will do!" I cried. "I choose this one!"

As I took a step toward her, I passed over the magic circle drawn on the floor.

"We have been robbed!"

The words went through my head a few times before I could understand them. It was my wife's voice. It sounded like a lullaby: "We have been robbed, robbed, robbed . . . ."

A vigorous shaking snapped me into alertness. I realized that I was lying on my back on the floor, with a small glass vial in my hand.

"We have been robbed!" Matilda repeated.

Through the fog in my brain, I began to remember the events of the night. There was the door through which my ghostly visitors had come. There was the chalk circle with the magical markings. But where was Mr. Abrahams? And what was this open window with the rope hanging out of it? And where were my silver tray and candlesticks?

I have never seen Mr. Abrahams or my valuables since. According to the police, Mr. Abrahams was none other than Jemmy Wilson, a notorious burglar. He must have overheard Jack Brocket searching for a ghost-hunter in the pub, and so he made his services available.

The mysterious, ghostly visitors I saw were explained to me by a doctor. He analyzed the remaining drops of "essence of Lucoptolycus." He determined the potion to be a strong sedative well known for causing visions. Because I had been expecting to see ghosts, my visions were perfectly ghostly.

Needless to say, I have gotten over my passion for ghosts.

19

A CREATURE OF HABIT

Ambrose Bierce

It should have been an ordinary hanging. Actually, the hanging part of it *was* ordinary. It's what happened after that was so strange.

The man they hanged was a gambler named Harry Graham. Most people called him "Gray Hank." He shot a man in a bar one day, after they got into an argument over a card game.

This was in Montana in 1865, a time and a place where people didn't think twice about taking the law into their own hands. Within an hour after the murder, the townspeople organized a trial and decided to hang Gray Hank for murder.

The hanging party threw a noose over a tree limb. They tied the free end to a bush. The noose was slipped over Hank's neck while he stood on the back of a horse.

At the snap of a whip, the horse sprang from under him, leaving Gray Hank's feet swinging eighteen inches from the ground. He hung there for exactly half an hour, and the crowd stayed to watch. Then doctors came forward and pronounced him dead. The rope was untied from the bush, and two men lowered the body.

As soon as its feet touched the ground, the corpse rushed into the crowd, trailing the rope behind. Its head rolled from side to side, its eyes stared, and its tongue stuck out. The dead man's face was ghastly purple, and the lips were covered with bloody froth.

With cries of horror, the crowd scattered. People stumbled and fell over one another. They pushed and bumped and shoved.

All the while, the horrible dead man pranced in and out among them – lifting his feet so high at each step that his knees struck his chest. His tongue was swinging like a panting dog's. Foam flew from his swollen lips. The deepening twilight added more terror to the scene, and men fled from the spot, not daring to look behind.

From out of this confusion appeared the tall figure of Dr. Arnold Spier. He was one of the physicians who pronounced the murderer dead. He moved directly toward the dead man, whose movements were a little slower and a little less jerky now.

Dr. Spier grabbed the corpse by the arms and laid it on its back. The body immediately became stiff and still.

"The dead are creatures of habit," explained Dr. Spier. "A corpse still on its feet will walk and run. But if you place it on its back, it will lie quietly."

MAN-SIZE IN MARBLE

Edith Nesbit

Although every word of this story is true, I do not expect people to believe it. I tell it to you as it happened. You be the judge.

It happened just a few years ago. Laura and I were on our honeymoon. We left our seaside resort to see a church in a little village to the south. The area was beautiful and quiet. As luck would have it, we found a cottage for sale near the church.

The cottage was a long, low building with rooms sticking out in unexpected places. It had been built around the remains of an old house that had once stood there. It was about two miles from the village. We decided to buy it.

I was a painter in those days, and Laura wrote poems and stories. We hired an old peasant woman named Mrs. Dorman to keep house. She was a great comfort to us. Besides doing housework, she amused us with stories of smugglers and highwaymen, and better yet, of eerie sights one could see on lonely starlit nights.

We had three months of happiness. Then one October evening, Mrs. Dorman suddenly announced that she had to leave at the end of the week. Something was troubling her.

"She was acting so strangely," said

Laura. "Could we have insulted her somehow?"

"I'll talk with her later," I replied. "Let's walk up to the church. That always makes you feel better."

We loved to visit the large and lonely church, especially on bright nights. The path leading to it wound through the woods, over the crest of a hill, and through two meadows before reaching the graveyard wall.

Inside, the arches rose into darkness. Moonlight filtered in through the rich stained-glass windows. On either side of the altar was a stone slab. On each slab lay a gray marble figure of a knight in full armor. Their hands were held in prayer. These life-size statues were the most peculiar objects in the church. The pale stone figures seemed to glow against the black oak of the rest of the church.

The names of the knights were forgotten, but the peasants said they had been fierce and wicked men. Their deeds were so foul that the house they lived in had been struck by lightning as a punishment from heaven. That house, by the way, had stood on the site of the cottage where Laura and I were living.

Looking at the hard faces of these stone figures, it was easy to believe the stories of evil. But for all their wickedness, their ancestors were rich enough to persuade the church to display the statues. Laura and I looked at the sleeping figures, rested awhile, and then went home.

Back at the cottage, I pressed Mrs. Dorman for the real reason she wanted to leave us.

"Have you any fault to find with us, Mrs. Dorman?" I asked.

"None at all, sir. You've been most kind, I'm sure."

"But why must you go this week? So suddenly?" I persisted.

"Well, sir," she said in a low and

hesitating voice, "you may have seen in the church them two shapes beside the altar."

"You mean the statues of the knights in armor," I said cheerfully.

"I mean them two bodies, drawed out man-size in marble." She paused to breathe a heavy sigh, then continued: "They do say that on Halloween, them two bodies sits up on their slabs, gets off, and then walks down the aisle. And as the church clock strikes eleven, they walks out of the church door, over the graves, and along the path. If it's a wet night, there's marks of their feet in the morning."

"And where do they go?" I asked, fascinated by this colorful legend.

"They comes back here to their home, sir. And if anyone meets them . . . ."

"Well, what then?" I asked.

But no. I couldn't get another word out of her—except for a warning.

"Whatever you do, sir, lock the door early on Halloween."

I didn't tell Laura about the legend. I feared it might upset her even though it was nonsense. I would talk about it the day it was over. On Thursday, October 30, Mrs. Dorman left. She promised to return to work the following week.

Friday—Halloween—came. Laura and I spent a pleasant day cleaning and doing work. But as the sun began to set, Laura's gay mood changed. "You are sad, my darling," I said.

"Not sad, exactly," she replied. "I'm uneasy. I shiver, but I'm not cold. I feel as if something evil will happen."

We sat in silence by the fire for a while. Laura grew a little more cheerful, but she looked pale and tired.

I craved my pipe before bed, but I didn't want to disturb Laura with the smoke. I told her I would take it outside.

"Don't stay out too long," she said.

"I won't, my deary," I replied, kissing her on the forehead.

I strolled out the front door, leaving it unlatched. The night was absolutely

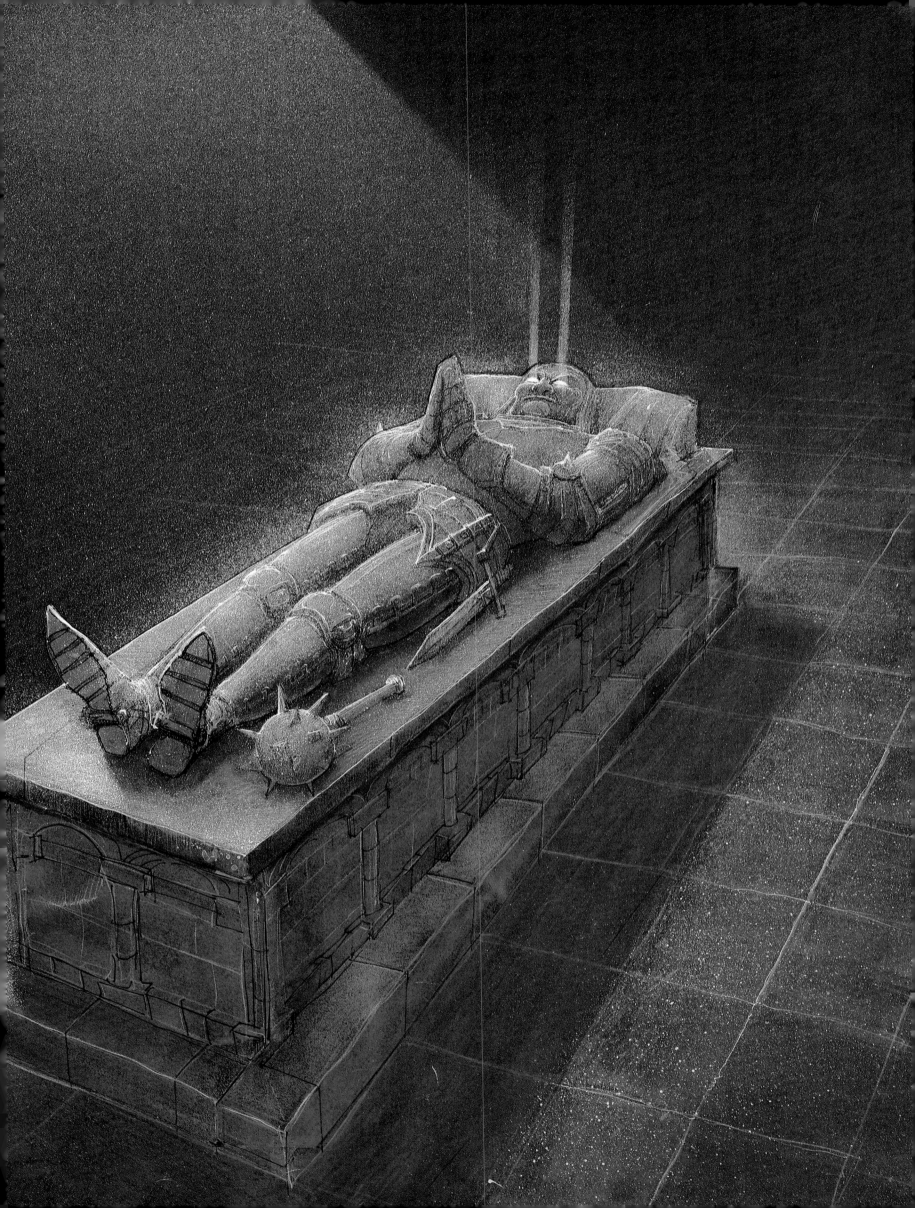

silent. Across the meadows I could see the church tower standing out black and gray against the sky. The bell chimed eleven. I didn't feel ready for bed yet. I would go up to the church. As I walked past the house, I could see Laura asleep in her chair by the fire.

I walked slowly along the edge of the woods. I distinctly heard a step in the dry leaves. But when I stopped, the sound stopped, too. It must have been an echo, I thought.

Approaching the church, I noticed that the door was open. Since Laura and I were the only ones who visited the church except on Sundays, I blamed myself for leaving it unlatched the other night.

I went in. I was halfway down the aisle before I remembered, with a sudden chill, that this was the very day and hour when the marble statues were supposed to walk.

I was ashamed of myself for feeling a moment of fear at the thought of the legend. I was glad I had come, because I could tell Mrs. Dorman how silly the legend was.

With my hands in my pockets, I passed up the dimly lit aisle. Just then the moon came out, throwing light into the church. I stopped short. My heart gave a leap that nearly choked me, and then sank sickeningly.

The marble knights were gone! I passed my hands over the slabs to be sure I wasn't seeing things. The slabs were smooth and flat. The figures *were* gone.

And then a horror seized me. Laura! I ran out of the church, biting my lips to keep from shrieking aloud. Just as I approached our cottage, a dark figure seemed to spring out of the ground. Mad with panic, I shouted, "Get out of my way, can't you!"

As I pushed by the figure, my arms were caught just above the elbows. It was Dr. Kelly, our nearest neighbor.

"Let me go, you fool," I gasped. "The marble figures have gone from the church!"

"You've been listening to too many old wives' tales," the doctor laughed.

"I've seen the bare slabs. I've got to get to my wife," I pleaded.

"Rubbish," said the doctor. "Come and show me the slabs. Don't be a coward."

The doctor's calm manner brought me back to my senses. We returned to the church and walked up the aisle. I shut my eyes, knowing the statues would not be there. I heard Dr. Kelly strike a match. "Here they are," he said cheerfully.

And there they were! I drew a deep breath and shook the doctor's hand.

"It must have been some trick of the light," I said sheepishly.

"No doubt," he replied.

He was leaning over and looking at the right-hand figure, who was the most evil-looking of the two.

"Look," said the doctor. "This one's hand is broken."

And so it was. I was certain that it had been perfect the last time Laura and I had been there. I was so relieved to see the statue that I didn't concern myself about the broken hand.

It was late. I invited Dr. Kelly to the cottage. As we approached, bright light streamed through the open front door. Had Laura gone out?

We glanced around the living room. At first we didn't see her. Her chair was empty and her book and handkerchief were on the floor.

Her body lay half on a table and half on the window seat. Her head hung down over the table, the brown hair falling to the carpet. Her lips were drawn back, and her eyes were wide, wide open. What had they seen last?

"It's all right, Laura! I've got you safe!" I cried. She fell into my arms in a heap. Her hands were tightly clenched. In one of them she held something. When I was quite sure she was dead, I let the doctor open her hand to see what she held.

It was a gray marble finger.

ROSE ROSE

Barry Pain

Sefton stepped back from his picture. "Rest now, please," he said. Miss Rose Rose, his model, threw a striped blanket around herself, stepped from the throne, and crossed the studio.

She was beautiful from the crown of her head to the soles of her feet. Every pose she took was graceful. She was the daughter of an artists' model, and had been working since childhood.

Rose Rose wasn't cultured, or businesslike, or educated. Modeling was all she knew, and she was the best. Once, she had held the same pose, without resting, for three solid hours.

While Rose Rose was getting dressed, Sefton flung himself into an easy chair and studied his painting. He was a man of forty, thick-set, round-faced, with a reddish moustache turned fiercely upward.

He was lucky to have Miss Rose model for him. She had exactly the right look for his painting of Aphrodite, the Greek goddess of love. But even though she was the most highly-paid model, she couldn't always be depended on to arrive at the studio on time.

On wintry mornings, when every hour of daylight was precious, she might be two hours late, or she might not show up at all. Still, her talents were so extraordinary that artists always came back to her.

"Can you be here tomorrow at nine?" asked Sefton to Rose Rose as she stepped from behind the changing-screen.

"A quarter past would be better," Rose replied.

"Well… all right," Sefton reluctantly agreed.

"I know what you're thinking, Mr. Sefton," said Rose Rose. "You think I don't mean to come tomorrow. You've been listening to Mr. Merion. All because I was late for him once. With good reason, too!"

"Mr. Merion recommended you to me, Miss Rose. But he suggested I never let you out of my sight. You *will* be here on time tomorrow, won't you?" urged the artist.

"You needn't worry about that," said Miss Rose, eagerly. "I'll be here a quarter past nine no matter what happens. Even if I die first! Is that good enough for you, Mr. Sefton?"

Despite Miss Rose's promise, he didn't feel sure of her.

The next morning, Sefton arrived at the studio at half past eight. He set out his paints and selected his brushes. As he studied the painting, he noticed that Aphrodite's face had a mocking expression.

It was just before nine when he found that he was out of cigarettes. He still had time to go to the shop around the corner. In case Rose Rose arrived while he was away, he left the studio door open.

Sefton figured that Rose Rose would be at least twenty minutes late. While he was at the shop, he bought a newspaper to occupy him as he waited. But on his return, he found his model already stepping onto the throne.

"Good morning, Miss Rose. You're a lady of your word."

Rose murmured a reply, but Sefton's mind was already on the painting.

The work went well, and Rose Rose showed no sign of tiring. Sefton worked for more than an hour before he realized Rose Rose should take a break.

"We'll have a rest now, Miss Rose," he said cheerily.

At that moment he felt the

unmistakable
touch of human fingers
drawn lightly across the
back of his neck. He spun
around with a sudden start. No
one was there. He turned back to
the throne. Rose Rose had vanished.

With great care he put down
his palette and brushes. He
said in a loud voice,
"Where are you, Miss
Rose?"

Silence hung in
the hot air of the studio.

He repeated the question
and got no answer. He stepped behind
the dressing-screen. Then a most terrifying thought struck him – his model had
never been there at all!

He sat down and tried to think of an explanation. He had been working very hard lately, he told himself. He was too wrapped up in the painting. He expected to see Rose Rose when he returned from the shop, so his mind told him she was there.

He couldn't convince himself. Nothing like this had ever happened before. The more he thought about it, the more frightened he became.

To calm his nerves, Sefton picked up the newspaper. Reading about day-to-day events would surely settle his nerves. Even so, he couldn't escape the fact that for the last hour he had done his most delicate work, and the model wasn't even there.

Sefton tried to focus on the newspaper. Then his eye fell on a paragraph headed "Motor Fatalities."

He read that Miss Rose Rose, an artists' model, had been struck by a car about seven o'clock the night before. She had died a short time after.

Sefton rose from his chair and opened a large pocketknife. He felt a mad impulse to slash the canvas to rags. He stopped before the painting. The face of Aphrodite smiled at him with an unearthly, eerie, but irresistible sweetness.

In the months that followed, Sefton allowed no one to visit him while he finished the painting. His friends wondered who his model was, since Rose was dead. Sefton refused to say.

Rose Rose kept her appointments with Sefton, even though she had to travel to the studio from beyond the grave.

As for the painting, it was an immediate success. It was found in Sefton's abandoned studio. The artist was never heard from again.

THE UPPER BERTH

F. Marion Crawford

I have sailed across the Atlantic pretty often. Like most old sailors, I have my favorite ships. The *Kamtschatka* was one of my favorites. But no longer. Nothing can make me take another voyage on her. I'll tell you why.

It was a warm morning in June when I last boarded the *Kamtschatka*. The steward greeted me and took my bags.

"Room 105, lower berth," said I.

A strange look washed over the steward's face. It made me nervous.

"Well, I'll be darned!" he said in a low voice, and he led the way.

The room was ordinary. It had plenty of space. Sand-colored curtains half-closed the empty upper berth. I had hoped to have the room to myself. Later that night, after we left the pier, I was disappointed to see that I was to have a companion.

The man wasn't in the room. I knew of him only because his suitcase was in the far corner, and his umbrella and a few more things lay on the upper berth. Before I had been in bed long, he entered. He was a very tall man, very thin, very pale, with sandy hair and whiskers, and gray eyes. I never saw him again after that first night in room 105.

I was sleeping soundly when I was suddenly awakened by a loud noise. I guessed that my roommate must have leaped from the upper berth to the floor. I heard him fumbling with the latch on the door. Then I heard his footsteps as he raced down the hallway, leaving the door open behind him.

The door swung on its hinges as the ship rolled. I got up to shut it, and groped my way back to my berth in the darkness. I went to sleep again, but I had no idea how long I slept.

When I awoke it was still dark. The air felt cold and damp. The cabin had a peculiar smell, as if it had been wet with sea water. I covered myself as best as I could and dozed off again. I could hear my roommate turn over in the upper berth. I thought I heard him groan, and suspected he was seasick. I slept till early daylight.

The ship was rolling heavily. The gray light coming through the porthole changed with every movement. It was terribly cold. To my surprise, the porthole was open and hooked back. I got up to shut it. Then I decided to dress. The damp smell of the night before had left the room. The curtains were drawn on the upper berth. My roommate was still asleep.

I went up on deck. The day was warm and cloudy, with an oily smell on the water. On the deck I met the ship's doctor.

"It's not much of a morning," said the doctor.

"It was very cold last night," I replied. "And my stateroom was damp, too."

"Damp?" said the doctor. "Where's your room?"

"One hundred and five."

To my surprise, the doctor shuddered.

"What's the matter?" I asked.

"Oh . . . nothing," he replied. "Only everyone's complained about that room for the last three trips. I believe there is something . . . well, it's not my business to frighten passengers."

"I'm not afraid of dampness," I replied.

"It's not just the dampness. But never mind," the doctor said. "Do you have a roommate?"

"Yes. He bolts out in the middle of the night and leaves the door open."

"Look," said the doctor, with a curious expression on his face, "I have a good-size cabin. Why don't you share it with me? It will be safer than sleeping in room 105."

"What are you talking about?" I said, surprised at his offer.

"On the last three trips, the people who have slept in room 105 have gone overboard," he answered gravely.

The news was startling. The look on the doctor's face told me he was serious. I thanked him for his offer, but told him I wanted to stay in my room.

After breakfast I returned to the room. The curtains on the upper berth were still drawn, so I assumed my roommate was still asleep. As I left the room, the steward stopped me and told me that the captain wanted to see me. I went to the captain's cabin and found him waiting for me.

"Your roommate has disappeared," he said. "We're afraid he's gone overboard."

"He's the fourth, then!" I exclaimed.

The captain seemed annoyed that I knew about the other three. He offered me my choice of any of the officers' cabins to sleep in for the rest of the journey. I replied that I'd rather have my original room, especially now that I had it to myself.

"Of course you have a right to stay where you are," said the captain. "But I wish you'd leave 105 and let me lock it up."

Towards evening I met the doctor again. He asked if I'd changed my mind about my room. I said I hadn't.

"Then you will before long," he said, very grimly.

I went to bed late that night. I couldn't help thinking of the man I shared my room with, now drowned and dead. I pulled back the curtains on the upper berth to be certain the man was gone.

As I undressed for bed, I noticed that the porthole was once again wide open. This made me angry, and I went to find Robert, the steward. I dragged him back to the room and demanded to know why he opened the porthole.

"If you please, sir," explained Robert, "nobody can keep this port shut at night. You can try it yourself. Look. Now I've fastened it tight, haven't I?"

I tried the porthole, and found it perfectly tight. Robert left and I went to bed, but I wasn't sleepy. I lay on my berth, looking at the moonlight through the porthole. I must have lain there for an hour. Just as I was dozing, I was roused by a blast of cold air and the spray of the sea on my face. The porthole was open and fastened back!

I rose and crossed the room to close the porthole. As I examined it, I heard something moving behind me in the upper berth. I turned to look, though I could see nothing in the darkness. I heard a very faint groan. Was someone there? I sprang across the room, tore the curtains of the upper berth aside, and thrust in my hands. There was someone.

From behind the curtains came a gust of wind that smelled horribly of stale sea water. I gripped something that had the shape of a man's arm, but was smooth, and wet, and icy cold. As I pulled, the creature sprang violently against me. It was a clammy, oozy mass, heavy and wet, but with terrible strength. I pulled myself away. In an instant, the door opened and the thing rushed out.

I rushed after the creature, but lost it around a corner. Frightened badly, I returned to the room. The whole place smelled of stale sea water. I examined the upper berth, expecting to find it drenched with sea water, but it was bone dry.

The porthole was open again. I closed it tight and bent the brass fitting. It would be impossible to open it again. I sat there all night, thinking about what had happened.

The morning dawned at last. I went on deck to enjoy the fresh air and to clear my head. The captain was there. I tried to explain the night's events. I told him I had been more scared than I had ever been in my life.

"Look here," he said, "I'll tell you what I'll do. I'll share your room myself, and we'll see what happens. I think we can find out between us."

Later that night, the captain and I went to my room. The ship's carpenter came and sealed the porthole tight. We checked the room carefully, and when we were satisfied, the captain and I locked ourselves in. He sat in front of the door. I sat on the edge of the lower berth.

"The first man who went overboard was a lunatic," explained the captain. "His friends didn't know he was aboard. On the next trip—what are you looking at?"

My eyes were riveted upon the porthole. The brass bolt was beginning to turn very slowly. Seeing where I was looking, the captain looked, too.

"It moves!" he gasped.

Just then, my reading lantern, which was in the upper berth, went out.

There was still light coming through the hall window. I got up to fix the lantern, and the captain jumped to his feet with a loud cry of surprise.

I turned quickly. He was wrestling with all his might against the porthole, which was beginning to move. I went to help him. The porthole suddenly sprang open, throwing us both to the floor.

"There's something in that berth!" cried the captain in a strange voice.

I pounced upon it. It was something ghastly, horrible beyond words. It was like the body of a man long drowned, and yet it moved and had the strength of ten men.

I gripped it with all my might—the slippery, oozy, horrible thing. Dead white eyes seemed to stare at me. It stank of foul sea water, and its shiny hair hung in awful, wet curls over its dead face. It began to overpower me. It wrapped its corpse's arms around my neck until I cried out and let it go.

The thing sprang across me and threw itself upon the captain. The captain was knocked down, dazed and horrified. The thing paused an instant, and then vanished through the porthole.

Well, do you want to hear more? There is nothing more.
The ship's carpenter nailed the door to room 105 shut.

If you ever take passage on the *Kamtschatka*,
you may ask for room 105. You will be
told that it is occupied. Yes, it is
occupied — by that dead
thing.

LOST HEARTS

M. R. James

Stephen Elliott had just turned eleven. He had been an orphan for six months when he came to live with his cousin, Mr. Abney.

Mr. Abney was a quiet, private old man. He was an expert on ancient religions, and he had written many articles on superstitions and myths from around the world. He was so wrapped up in his studies, his neighbors were surprised that he had even heard of his orphan cousin. They were even more surprised that Mr. Abney wished to adopt him.

It was a crisp September evening when Stephen arrived at his new home. Mr. Abney cheerfully greeted his young cousin. After they talked for awhile, Mr. Abney directed his housekeeper, Mrs. Bunch, to fix the boy's supper.

Mrs. Bunch and Stephen became great friends. She had worked for Mr. Abney for twenty years, and she answered all of Stephen's questions about the house and Mr. Abney. She made Stephen feel as comfortable as possible.

One evening, Stephen was sitting by the fire with Mrs. Bunch.

"Is Mr. Abney a good man, and will he go to heaven?" he suddenly asked.

"Good?" said the housekeeper. "Master's as kind a soul as I ever did see. Didn't I tell you of the little boy he took in from the street? And the little girl, too?"

"No. Do tell me about them, Mrs. Bunch," urged Stephen.

"Well," said Mrs. Bunch, "I don't remember much about the little girl. Mr. Abney brought her home two years after I began working here.

"The poor little girl was an orphan. She lived here three weeks. And then one morning she ran away before any of us awoke. No one's seen her since."

"And what about the little boy?" asked Stephen.

"Ah! That poor boy!" sighed Mrs. Bunch. "Master found him about

seven years ago. He was a foreigner, all alone in the world. He stayed a while and then he was off one morning just like the girl. No sign of him after that."

That night, Stephen had a curious dream. Down the hall from his bedroom was an unused bathroom. It was kept locked, but the door had a curtainless window in it. Through the door could be seen an old bathtub below a window on the far wall.

Stephen dreamed that he was looking through the bathroom door. Moonlight was shining through the outside window. Lying in the tub was a thin, gray-faced girl wrapped in a burial cloth. Her thin lips were twisted into a faint and dreadful smile. Her hands were pressed tightly over her heart.

As Stephen watched, the figure moaned and began to move its arms. The terror of the sight woke Stephen. He found himself standing in front of the bathroom door. With remarkable courage, he peeked through the window to see if the figure of his dream was really there. It wasn't. Stephen went back to bed.

The following evening, Mrs. Bunch was in the pantry and Stephen was playing nearby. Mr. Parkes, the butler, rushed in with some news for Mrs. Bunch. He didn't see Stephen.

"Master Abney can get his own wine, if he wants, Mrs. Bunch," blurted the butler. "I'm not going back to the wine cellar. Something's down there. I'd like to say it's rats, but I think it's worse than that. I could hear them talking."

"Such nonsense, Mr. Parkes!" replied Mr. Bunch. "You'll frighten Master Stephen with talk like that."

"What! Master Stephen!" said Parkes, noticing the boy for the first time. "Stephen knows when I'm playing a joke on you, Mrs. Bunch."

But Stephen could tell by the look on Parkes's face that the butler wasn't joking.

It was the first day of spring, a windy, noisy day in March. At lunch, Mr. Abney told Stephen that he had something important to discuss. But since he had a busy day ahead, he asked Stephen to come to his study at eleven o'clock that night. He told Stephen not to mention the appointment to Mrs. Bunch or to anyone else.

Stephen was excited about staying up that late. He looked in at the study on his way upstairs that evening and saw a grill in front of the fireplace, an old silver cup of wine, and some sheets of paper with writing on them. Mr. Abney was sprinkling some incense onto the grill from a round silver box as Stephen passed.

About ten o'clock, Stephen was standing at the open window of his bedroom, looking over the countryside. The wind was filled with ghostly sounds. Just as he was thinking of shutting the window, Stephen spotted two figures standing below. They were a boy and a girl, standing side by side, looking up at the window.

With a chill, Stephen recognized the girl from his dream. She stood still, half smiling, with her hands clasped over her heart.

The boy was more terrifying. He was thin, with black hair and ragged clothes. He raised his arms in the air with a look of menace and longing.

Stephen could see that the left side of his chest, where his heart should have been, was a gaping, black hole. Stephen began to hear the most awful and pitiful cry. But it wasn't exactly a sound. It was more like a feeling in Stephen's brain. It was a hungry, lonely sound that filled Stephen's head. In another moment, the dreadful figures moved swiftly and noiselessly over the dry gravel and vanished.

Horribly frightened, Stephen took his candle and hurried to Mr. Abney's study. It was almost time for their meeting. He knocked on the door, but there was no answer. Terrified and frantic, Stephen pushed on the door, but it wouldn't move.

Then he heard Mr. Abney try to cry out, but the cry was choked in his throat. Why? Had he, too, seen the mysterious children? Now everything was quiet. The door swung open.

Stephen found Mr. Abney in his chair. His head was thrown back, and his face had a look of rage, fright, and terrible pain. On the left side of his chest was a deep, black hole where his heart should have been. His hands were clean, and there was no blood on the long knife that lay on his desk.

The window was open. The police decided that Mr. Abney had probably been killed by a wild animal. But years afterward, Stephen Elliott discovered the truth about the death of his cousin.

When Stephen was grown and living on his own, he received a letter from Mrs. Bunch, who was now an old woman. The letter said only, "I didn't know, Stephen. How could I have known?"

Enclosed with the letter were pages from Mr. Abney's diary. As Stephen read them, his blood turned to ice. "I have discovered the ancient secret of eternal life," the diary began. "It requires the sacrifice of three children on the first day of spring. Their hearts must be removed while they are still alive, and burned to ashes on a grill. The ashes are mixed with wine, and then drunk."

Stephen couldn't believe what he was reading, but he couldn't put the papers down.

"I have already killed a little girl, whose body I hid in the old bathroom," wrote Mr. Abney. "And also a young foreign boy, whom I buried in the wine cellar. My next — and final — sacrifice will be my cousin, Stephen Elliott. Then I will live forever!"

Stephen trembled as he put down the pages. He remembered the two figures he saw under his window as a child. They were the murdered children, who came back to save Stephen's life.

THE LEGEND OF SLEEPY HOLLOW
Washington Irving

In the eastern shore of the Hudson River, nestled in upstate New York, lies a small village known as Tarry Town. And not two miles from this village is a little valley that is one of the quietest places in the whole world. A small brook glides through it with just a murmur. The occasional whistle of a quail or the tapping of a woodpecker are the only sounds to break the silence. This tranquil place has long been known as Sleepy Hollow.

Some say the place is bewitched, causing the residents of Sleepy Hollow to fall into trances and see visions or hear music or voices in the air. Nightmares are frequent among the residents, and the local lore is rich with peculiar stories, strange superstitions, and tales of hauntings.

The most horrible spirit that haunts the region is a horseman without a head. He is believed to have been a soldier whose head was carried away by a cannonball. He is seen by the country folk as he hurries along in the gloom of night, searching for his head. He is known as the Headless Horseman.

One fateful year, a schoolteacher named Ichabod Crane moved to Tarry Town from Connecticut. He was tall and exceedingly thin, with narrow shoulders, hands that dangled a mile out of their sleeves, and feet that looked more like shovels. His head was small, with huge ears, a spindle neck, and a long beak of a nose. To see him in the distance on a windy day, with his clothes fluttering, you'd think he was a scarecrow.

Ichabod stayed with each family of Tarry Town for a week at a time. In exchange for food and shelter, he would do chores and tell stories. He especially loved stories of ghosts and witchcraft. After school, he would lie in a bed of clover and read these monstrous tales to himself until the light faded.

Then, as he walked through the woods to whichever farmhouse he was staying at, his imagination would run wild. In the gathering gloom, every rustling leaf would become a spirit sneaking up on him. Every firefly, a demon eye. To Ichabod, the caws and twitters of the birds were like screams of the undead. He dared not look over his shoulder for fear of what might be gaining on him.

To draw himself away from these thoughts, Ichabod would sing psalms, which would drift through the air of Sleepy Hollow.

People enjoyed his singing so much that he was persuaded to give lessons. His favorite student was Katrina Van Tassel, the daughter of a very wealthy farmer. She was a young woman of eighteen, with rosy cheeks and winning ways. Ichabod imagined what a wonderful wife she would make, and how doubly wonderful it would be to inherit her father's beautiful farm.

But Ichabod wasn't alone in his admiration of Katrina. The lady was also being courted by a burly, broad-shouldered man named Brom Bones. Brom was the hero of the county. Rough but good-natured, he seemed to be at the center of every game and prank. He and his gang of four friends could be heard dashing past the farmhouses at midnight, whooping and hollering at the tops of their lungs. Neighbors looked at Brom with awe and admiration.

Most men would have shrunk away from a such a rival

as Brom Bones. But not Ichabod Crane. Ichabod was in love with Katrina and he thought of every excuse to be with her.

Brom was too proud to attack Ichabod directly. Instead he made Ichabod the butt of many practical jokes. One time, Brom stopped up the chimney in Ichabod's schoolhouse so that it filled with smoke. Another time he turned the furniture topsy-turvy. The poor schoolmaster began to think all the witches in the country held their meetings there.

These antics went on for some time. Then one fine afternoon, Ichabod was handed an invitation to a party at the farmhouse of Katrina's father. Ichabod spent an extra hour getting ready. He dusted off his only suit for the occasion. He even borrowed a horse so he could ride to the festivities in style. It didn't matter to him that the horse was bony and broken-down.

Ichabod arrived at the party toward evening, and the Van Tassel mansion was brimming with food, music, and merriment. Ichabod and Katrina danced while Brom Bones sat by himself, brooding in a corner.

After the dance, Ichabod mingled with the other guests. He was attracted to a group of folks who were exchanging wild and wonderful legends of Sleepy Hollow.

The favorite topic was,

of course, the headless horseman. He had lately been seen patrolling the countryside. It was said that he tethered his horse among the graves in the old churchyard. The old whitewashed church was nestled in the woods beside a large, grassy dell and a swift, violent stream. A wooden bridge led from the road to the church. The bridge was thickly shaded by overhanging trees. It was gloomy by day, and fearfully dark at night. Here was the favorite haunt of the headless horseman.

One old man, a firm disbeliever in ghosts, told how he rode behind the horseman until they reached the bridge. There the horseman suddenly turned into a skeleton, threw the old man into the brook, and sprang away over the treetops with a clap of thunder.

Brom Bones, who could outdo any story, told how he offered to race the horseman for a bowl of punch. Brom would have won, but just as the racers came to the church bridge, the horseman vanished in a flash of fire.

It was midnight, the witching hour, when Ichabod began his lonely ride back to Tarry Town. The night grew darker and darker. All the stories of ghosts and goblins came crowding into Ichabod's mind.

In the center of the road stood an enormous tulip tree. It towered like a giant above the other trees. Its fantastic, gnarled limbs twisted almost to the ground, then rose into the air again.

As Ichabod approached this fearful tree, he began to whistle. He thought his whistle was answered, but it was only a breeze through the dry branches. As he crept closer, he thought he saw something ghostly hanging in the center of the tree. It was only a scar caused by lightning.

Suddenly he heard a groan. His teeth chattered and his knees gripped the saddle. But it was only two boughs rubbing past each other.

He passed the tree in safety, but new perils lay before him.

Ichabod had gone just a short way when his sharp ears picked up a slight sound. In a dark shadow beside the road, he saw something huge, black, and towering. It did not move, but seemed like some gigantic monster ready to spring.

Ichabod felt his hair rise on his head. It was too late to turn and flee. He began to sing a psalm tune. At that instant, the shadowy object moved into his path.

In the gloom, Ichabod saw that the shape appeared to be a large horseman mounted on a powerful black horse. The stranger rode beside Ichabod, exactly matching his pace.

The stranger's silence was unbearable. Ichabod tried to continue his psalm tune, but his mouth had gone dry with fear. The pair rode along. Ichabod tried to pretend he didn't see the stranger.

Then they came to the top of a hill and into the moonlight. Ichabod could see that his fellow traveler was truly gigantic in height and wrapped in a cloak. Ichabod was horror-struck when he saw that the stranger was also headless! Instead of wearing his head on his shoulders, the stranger carried it on his saddle!

Ichabod's terror rose. He kicked at his horse, hoping to give his companion the slip, but the phantom galloped after him.

Away they dashed, through thick and thin, stones flying and sparks flashing at every bound. Ichabod stretched his long, lank body over his horse's head in his eagerness to flee.

They reached the road that turned off to Sleepy Hollow. But Ichabod's horse suddenly made an opposite turn, which took the terrified schoolteacher down to the dark bridge that led to the whitewashed church.

Still the horseman pursued, drawing closer and closer. When Ichabod was halfway through the hollow, his saddle straps gave way, and he could feel the saddle slipping from under him. He tried to hold on, but he could not. He saved himself by grasping his horse around its neck just as the saddle fell to the ground. He heard it trampled underfoot by the headless horseman.

Ichabod held his horse's neck for dear life. It was all he could do to stay on. An opening in the trees showed him that the church bridge was nearby. "There's the spot where the horseman disappears!" thought Ichabod. "If I can just reach that bridge, I am safe!"

Just then he heard the black steed panting and blowing close behind him. He even fancied that he felt his hot breath. Another kick in the ribs, and Ichabod's old horse sprang upon the bridge. He thundered over the wooden planks and reached the opposite side.

Now Ichabod dared to look behind to see if the headless horseman should vanish in a flash of fire, according to the stories. But instead he saw the monster rising in his stirrups, hurling his head at him. Ichabod tried to dodge the gruesome object, but too late. It hit Ichabod on the head with a tremendous crash. He tumbled into the dust as the black steed and its phantom rider passed by like a whirlwind.

Ichabod was never seen again. All that remained to tell the tale were the deep hoofprints on the road, Ichabod's hat, and close beside it a shattered pumpkin.

Shortly after Ichabod's disappearance, Brom Bones married Katrina Van Tassel. Whenever someone spoke of Ichabod's strange disappearance, a satisfied look would cross Brom's face. He would always burst into a hearty laugh at the mention of the pumpkin. Some suspected he knew more about the matter than he chose to tell.

the end ?

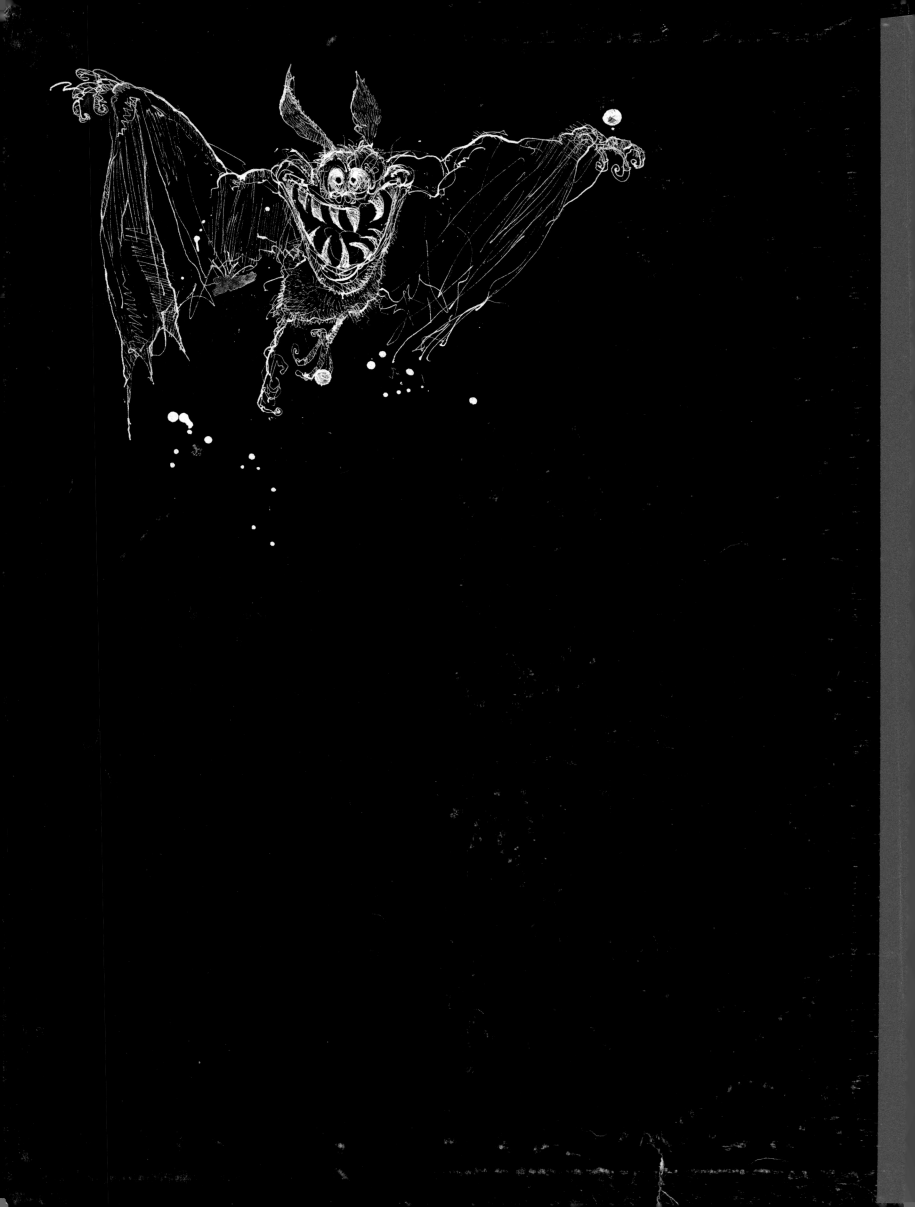